Karen's Haircut

**Here are some other books
about Karen
that you might enjoy:**

Little Sister

Karen's Haircut
Ann M. Martin

Illustrations by Susan Tang

A
LITTLE APPLE
PAPERBACK

SCHOLASTIC INC.
New York Toronto London Auckland Sydney

ISBN 0-590-42670-2

24 23 22 21 20 19 18 17 16 15 14 13   5/9

Printed in the U.S.A.   40

First Scholastic printing, June 1990

*This book
is in honor of the birth of
Maxwell Joseph Lieb*

1

The Ugly Duckling

"Oh, I am a lovely, lovely lady," I sang.

"Me, too," said Nancy. "Would you like to have some tea?"

"Why, certainly. Lovely ladies must always have tea in the afternoon."

I am Karen Brewer. I just turned seven years old. My friend Nancy Dawes is seven, too. Nancy lives next door to my mother's house. She and I like to play lovely ladies and get dressed up. Nancy has pretty good dress-up clothes. So do I.

It was a Friday afternoon. I was over at

Nancy's, and boy, were we dressed up. We were the loveliest of lovely ladies. We sat down to tea at the little table in Nancy's room. We arranged her tea set. Nancy does not have any brothers or sisters. When she gets out her tea set, she does not have to worry about anyone messing it up. Over at my house, I have a little brother named Andrew. He is going on five. Sometimes he messes up my things.

At our tea party that day, Nancy was wearing blue high-heeled shoes, a long white slip, a straw hat, and nine necklaces. I was wearing red high heels, a long blue blouse, an apron, and a bride's veil.

"Yum, this tea is certainly delicious," I said.

"Scrumptious," added Nancy.

"Well, thank you very much for having me to tea, Miss Dawes. I better be going. I have to do some shopping. I need nail polish and hair curlers."

"May I come with you, Miss Brewer?"

asked Nancy. "I need nail polish and hair curlers, too."

"Why, of course you may come," I replied.

Nancy and I clomped through her house. Our high heels bumped along. We clomped into the living room.

"What lovely ladies!" exclaimed Nancy's mother.

We clomped into the kitchen. We clomped down the hallway.

"I think the store is in the bathroom," I said.

"Yes, I believe you are right," replied Lovely Lady Nancy.

So we clomped into the bathroom. I stopped in front of the standing long mirror. I looked at myself carefully. I was dressed up — but my clothes couldn't hide my glasses. They couldn't hide my two front teeth, either. Those teeth used to be smaller. Then they fell out. When the grown-up teeth came in, they were huge. They looked like rabbit teeth. Plus, two of my side teeth on the top were loose. I hate loose teeth. But when they come out, I hate the spaces they leave even more.

"I wish I were prettier," I said to Nancy.

"What's wrong with you?" she asked.

"Well, just look at me. I've got glasses, rabbit teeth, and loose teeth."

"I think you look fine," said Nancy.

But I did not agree.

I am an ugly duckling, I thought.

Suddenly, lovely ladies did not seem like such a fun game. I did not *feel* like a lovely lady. I was glad when Mommy called and said I had to come home. It was time for Andrew and me to go to Daddy's for the weekend.

2

Little House, Big House

I live at two houses — Mommy's house and Daddy's house. Both of them are in Stoneybrook, Connecticut. Why do I live at two houses? Because Mommy and Daddy are divorced. This is what happened: A long time ago, Mommy and Daddy decided they didn't want to live together anymore. After the divorce, they each got married again. Mommy married Seth. She and Seth live in a little house, which is the way they like things. Daddy married Elizabeth, who has

6

four children. They live in a big, huge house — a mansion. Daddy is a millionaire.

Now Andrew and I live mostly with Mommy and Seth. But every other weekend, and for two weeks during the summer, we live with Daddy and his big family.

Since Andrew and I go back and forth between the little house and the big house, we have two of almost everything — one at each house. We have bicycles at each house. I have a stuffed cat at each house. (One is named Goosie, the other is named Moosie.) I even ripped Tickly, my special blanket, in half so that I could have a piece at each house. With clothes and toys and other important things at each house, Andrew and I hardly have to pack at all when we go to Daddy's.

You know what else? I have a best friend at each house. My little-house best friend is Nancy. My big-house best friend is named Hannie Papadakis. She lives across the street from Daddy and one house down. Hannie

and Nancy and I are all in Ms. Colman's second-grade class at Stoneybrook Academy.

Guess what I call Andrew and me. I call us two-twos. I am Karen Two-Two and Andrew is Andrew Two-Two. That's because we have two of everything — mommies, daddies, friends, houses, and more. I got the name from a book Ms. Colman read to our class. It's called *Jacob Two-Two Meets the Hooded Fang*.

Here's who lives at the little house besides Andrew and me: Mommy, Seth (my stepfather), Rocky, Midgie, and Emily Junior. Rocky is Seth's cat. Midgie is his dog. Emily Junior is my rat. (You'll find out who she's named for in just a minute.)

Here's who lives at the big house besides Andrew and me: first of all, Daddy and Elizabeth (my stepmother) and Elizabeth's kids (my stepbrothers and stepsister). They are Charlie and Sam, who are so old they're in high school, David Michael, who is seven like me, and Kristy. I just love Kristy. She is one of my favorite people in the whole wide world. Kristy is thirteen and she baby-sits. She baby-sits for Andrew and me and lots of other kids. She baby-sits so much that she and her friends formed a business called the Baby-sitters Club. Kristy is the president.

Second, Emily Michelle and Nannie live at the big house. Emily Michelle is two years old. She is my adopted sister. Daddy and Elizabeth adopted her. She came from a far, faraway country called Vietnam. And she's the one I named my rat after. Nannie is my step-grandmother. I love her a lot, too. Nannie helps take care of Emily Michelle when everyone else is either at work or at school.

Oh, yes. Shannon and Boo-Boo live at the big house, too. Shannon is David Michael's puppy. Boo-Boo is Daddy's fat, old cat. I don't like him very much, and he doesn't like anyone except Daddy and Shannon.

Boo-Boo scratches and bites and hisses.

Boo-Boo is the only bad thing about the big house, though. I just love going to Daddy's. I like being with all those people. The big house is usually exciting.

Maybe, I thought, I could forget about being an ugly duckling while I was at the big house.

3

Professor

When Mommy drops Andrew and me off at the big house on Fridays, she usually calls, "See you later, alligators!"

Sometimes one of us answers, "After awhile, crocodile!"

On this Friday I yelled, "Not if I see you first!"

Mommy and Andrew and I laughed. Then Mommy waited in the car to see that we got inside Daddy's house safely. When the front door opened, I waved to Mommy. She drove away. Andrew and I would see her again late Sunday afternoon when she picked us up.

The person who had opened the door was Kristy. Yea!

"Hi, Kristy!" I cried.

"Hi," said Kristy with a grin. She let Andrew and me inside. She closed the door behind us. Then she gave us each a tight hug.

Soon everyone in my whole big-house family had gathered in the hallway. There were Daddy, Elizabeth, Nannie, Charlie, Sam, David Michael, Emily Michelle, and, of course, Kristy. Even Shannon came in. She pressed her wet nose into my hand. Boo-Boo did not show up, but I didn't care.

Everyone was hugging and kissing. Daddy swept first me and then Andrew up into his arms. When he put me down, David Michael said cheerfully to me, "Hi, Professor!"

He calls me that because of my glasses. "Professor" is not a mean nickname. It's a nice one. David Michael is usually a pain,

13

but sometimes he can be nice, and he was being nice when I first got my glasses and he said he thought they made me look smart — like a professor.

But that night I did not want to look like a smart professor. I wanted to look gorgeous. I wanted someone to say, "Hi, beautiful," to me. Only no one did.

I was feeling like an ugly duckling again, but I did not tell anyone.

I just love evenings at the big house when everyone is home. Those evenings are so busy and noisy. That night we ate dinner at the long, long table. We need a long table since nine people have to sit at it. (Emily sits in a high chair.) Nannie had fixed chicken and salad and corn for supper.

"You know what corn is, don't you, Andrew?" said Sam.

"A begetable," replied Andrew proudly.

"No. Corn is yellow teeth that have fallen out of old people's mouths."

"Ew, gross!" cried Andrew. "Nannie,

why are you making us eat old teeth?"

"Sam is teasing you, honey," said Nannie gently. Then she gave Sam a *look*.

I tried to laugh, but I couldn't. Even though the tooth joke was funny, all I could think about was being an ugly duckling.

When dinner was over, I helped Daddy and Elizabeth clean up the kitchen. Then Andrew, David Michael, Emily Michelle, and I played hide-and-seek. I had to help Emily a lot. She does not understand the game. When it's her turn to hide, she just sits and watches the rest of us.

We had finished playing hide-and-seek when Hannie called.

"Want to come over tomorrow?" she asked.

"Sure!" I replied. "Thanks."

Soon it was time to go to bed. I brushed my teeth with Andrew and David Michael. Then I changed into my pajamas. Kristy read me a bedtime story about a fairy princess.

I still felt like an ugly duckling.

4

The Loose Tooth

On Saturday morning I woke up slowly.
I like to lie around in my bed and think. I
hugged Moosie and Tickly and wondered
what Hannie and I would do at her house
that day.

While I was wondering, I explored my
mouth with my finger. There were those
awful loose teeth. One of them was quite a
bit looser than the other. I could push it
way back and forth. It was almost ready to
come out. What if it came out while I was

eating and I *swallowed* it? Oh, ew. Yuck. I had to get rid of that tooth.

I jumped out of bed, got dressed, and put on my glasses. I made my bed quickly. Then I ran downstairs. I was very nervous about that tooth.

At breakfast, I tried to eat my cereal with one hand and hold the tooth in place with the other. It was difficult — and messy.

"Karen!" said Elizabeth when she noticed. "What are you doing?"

"Holding onto my tooth," I told her. "I don't want to swallow it."

"I don't think you need to worry about that," said Daddy.

I wasn't so sure.

When breakfast was over, Sam said to me, "Karen, I can get your tooth out in a jiffy. I know lots of ways."

"You do?" I replied. Could I believe Sam? After all, he had told Andrew that corn kernels were old teeth.

"Sure," replied Sam. "I can yank it out with pliers."

18

"NO!" I cried.

"Or *you* can hold onto the tooth, and I'll pull your hand out of your mouth."

"NO!"

"All right. There's only one way left. I'll tie a string around your tooth. Very carefully," he added. "And I'll tie the other end of the string to a doorknob. Then I'll slam the door closed, and *bam!* Your tooth will come out. It will fly through the air on the string."

Well, that sounded pretty interesting. I had never seen one of my teeth fly through the air on a string.

"Okay," I told Sam. "You can tie my tooth up."

Sam got some string and a pair of scissors. Then we went to my room. I sat on my bed. It took awhile, but finally Sam tied the string around my loose tooth. Then he unrolled a long piece of string and cut it off. He tied the other end to the doorknob.

"Now you stay right there," said Sam, "while I slam the door."

"Is this going to hurt?" I asked.

"Maybe just for a second."

Sam put his hand on the door. "Okay," he said. "One . . . two . . ."

"STOP!" I cried. "Forget it. I don't want you to slam the door."

Sam took his hand away. "Are you sure?" he asked.

I nodded.

"Okay." Sam untied my tooth. "Cluck, cluck, cluck, cluck . . . CHICKEN!" he cried.

I didn't care. I told Daddy about my tooth. And you know what? Daddy got a Kleenex and pulled it out — just like that! It didn't hurt a bit, but it did bleed a little. Elizabeth helped me rinse out my mouth with salty water.

I looked at myself in the bathroom mirror. Yuck. Now I had glasses, rabbit teeth, one loose tooth, and a hole in my mouth where the other tooth had been.

Ugly duckling, ugly duckling, I thought.

But at least I could leave my tooth under my pillow for the Tooth Fairy that night.

The Other Loose Tooth

It was time to go to Hannie's house.

I crossed the street carefully, ran across the Papadakises' front lawn, and rang their doorbell.

Hannie answered it.

"Hi," I said. "Notice anything different about me?" I grinned broadly.

"Oh!" cried Hannie. "Your tooth finally came out." She let me inside.

"Yup," I said. "And look how loose *this* one is." I wiggled the other tooth back and forth with my tongue.

22

"*Ew,*" said Hannie. "Gross."

I smiled. I was teasing Hannie. She doesn't like loose teeth any more than I do.

"Well," said Hannie, "what do you want to do today?"

"Let's play tag!" I suggested. "We could get Andrew, David Michael, and Linny to play with us." (Linny is Hannie's older brother. He and David Michael are friends.)

"Okay," said Hannie.

So we found the boys, and then we began running around Hannie's backyard. Andrew was It first. He took forever tagging someone. Maybe that's because his legs are shorter than anyone else's.

He finally caught Hannie. Then Hannie was It. Hannie tagged me.

At last *I* was It. I love being It.

I ran all over Hannie's yard. First I went after Linny. I almost tagged him, but suddenly I changed my course. I turned around and ran after Hannie. Then I changed course again. This was to confuse everybody. When they were good and mixed up, I went after

David Michael. Since he was sure that I would change direction, he wasn't running very fast. But when he saw that I really *was* after him, he sped up.

I sped up, too.

I was running as fast as I'd ever run.

I stretched out my hand. "Tag . . . you're . . . *It!*" I cried. I stretched my arm out so far to tag him that I lost my balance and fell down.

"Oof!" I said. Then, "Oh! Oh, no!" I had fallen on my mouth, and — yes, my tooth had come out. My other loose tooth was rattling around in my mouth. I don't think it had been ready to come out, but it was out anyway.

"What's wrong?" cried Hannie. She ran over to me. The boys crowded around, too.

"I lost the other tooth," I said. I spit it into my hand.

My mouth was bleeding again.

"Gross!" said Linny. "That is so disgusting."

But Hannie said, "Come on inside. Mommy will fix your mouth."

So Hannie and I went into the Papadakises' kitchen, and Mrs. Papadakis patted at the empty space in my mouth with a Kleenex. Then she gave me a glass of salty water — just like Elizabeth had done — and I rinsed until there was no more blood.

"Hey!" said Hannie. "Tonight you'll put *two* teeth under your pillow for the Tooth

Fairy. I wonder if you get anything special for losing two teeth in one day."

"Maybe," I said. I wanted to go home. I had just peeked at myself in the bathroom mirror and I looked . . . like a freak. I had rabbit teeth, and gaps in my mouth everywhere, and my darn old glasses.

I was the ugliest duckling of all.

But I didn't want to be a baby, so when Hannie said, "Let's play tag again. The boys are still here," I said, "Okay."

It was the last thing I wanted to do.

6

Hannie's Wedding

The boys were still at the Papadakises' all right, but guess what. They were tired of tag. They were in the driveway, pretending they were space invaders.

"Grrrr. I am an alien," said Andrew to Hannie and me. "I will eat you up."

"And I will blast you with my ray gun," said Linny, pointing a stick at us.

I looked at Hannie. She looked at me.

"Let's go to my room and play," she said. (Hannie's collection of dress-up clothes is almost as good as Nancy's and mine.)

"Yeah," I said. I do not like playing space invaders.

Plus, my mouth hurt.

When we reached Hannie's room, she opened a trunk. Her father had made the trunk especially for her. He had written HANNIE on top, and painted bears and balloons around the sides. In the trunk are old hats and shoes and gloves and dresses, plus a cowgirl suit, a ballerina's tutu, and a police officer's uniform.

"Shall we be lovely ladies?" asked Hannie in a lovely-lady voice.

"But of course," I replied.

We put on dresses. We put on hats. We put on scarves and gloves and jewelry. Then we walked out of Hannie's room. We looked at ourselves in the long mirror in her parents' bedroom.

"Blecch," I said.

I turned around and marched back to Hannie's room. I took off my lovely-lady clothes and put them in her trunk.

Hannie watched me. "What's wrong?" she asked.

"I'm not a lovely lady," I told her.

"Neither am I," said Hannie. "We're just pretending."

"No, I mean I am not pretty. I am not even cute. I am an ugly duckling."

Hannie frowned.

"*Look* at me," I said. I pointed out all the ugly things.

"Hmm," said Hannie. "Maybe you'd feel better if you got your hair cut or something.

Maybe you need a change."

"I asked Mommy and Daddy if I could get contact lenses instead of glasses, and they both said, 'No. Not until you're fourteen.' "

"*Fourteen!*" cried Hannie. "You won't be fourteen for years."

"I know."

"Well, what about a new haircut? I like your hair the way it is now, but wouldn't it be exciting to go to a beauty parlor and get a haircut? Something new and special and different?"

"Yeah!" I exclaimed. Beauty parlors are terrific. Once I went on an ocean cruise on a huge ship. On the ship were swimming pools and restaurants and even a beauty parlor. And I went to the beauty parlor *by myself* and got a manicure.

"Maybe," I said excitedly to Hannie, "I could have my nails done, too. I would like them painted pink."

"Well, there's a new beauty parlor in

town," Hannie told me. "It's called Gloriana's House of Hair. Maybe you could go there."

"Yeah!" I cried. "I'll ask Daddy about it when I go home."

"You know what?" said Hannie. "This is perfect, because Scott and I are getting married soon. After your beauty treatment you will look *so* lovely. Then you can be the bridesmaid in our wedding." (Hannie is in love with Scott Hsu, a new boy who moved in down the street from us. He does not go to our school.)

"Thanks," I said, "but I thought you wanted me to be the photographer at your wedding."

"I did. But I want you to be a beautiful bridesmaid even more."

"Can you wait until after my beauty treatment?" I asked.

"Sure," replied Hannie. "No problem. The wedding is not scheduled yet."

"Goody! I can't wait!" I exclaimed.

Waiting for Tuesday

That afternoon, I left Hannie's. I had stayed for lunch. Hannie's father had fixed fruit salad for us. Yum. Strawberries are my favorites. You know what Andrew calls them? He calls them "strawbabies"!

When it was time for me to go home, Mrs. Papadakis gave me a little white box. "Your tooth is in here," she told me.

"Thank you," I replied.

I ran to my house.

"Look, everybody!" I cried. "I lost my other tooth at Hannie's! Here it is! Now I can put *two* teeth under my pillow for the Tooth Fairy."

My family was impressed.

"What do you think happens if you lose two teeth in one day?" I asked them.

"I think," replied Sam, "that the Tooth Fairy says to herself, 'Hmm. Karen is so lucky to have lost two teeth at once. I guess she doesn't need a surprise under her pillow. She has already had enough excitement.' "

"Sa-*am!*" I cried.

Later on, I found Daddy out in the herb garden. He was weeding it. No one else was in the backyard. It was a good time to ask him about getting a beauty treatment at Gloriana's House of Hair.

"Daddy?" I said. I sat down at the edge of the garden.

"Yes?" Daddy was hoeing. He stopped, leaned on the hoe, and looked at me.

"Daddy, I feel like an ugly duckling. My teeth are awful. I've got these big rabbit teeth in front, and the holes where my other

33

teeth fell out, and I have to wear glasses. Could I please, please, *please* get my hair cut? At Gloriana's House of Hair? It's a new place in town."

"I don't know," Daddy replied. "A fancy beauty salon?"

"Puh-*lease?* I just know I'll feel better with a new haircut . . . and a manicure . . . and a pedicure. Pink toenails would look so, so lovely."

"I think a haircut and a manicure will be enough," said Daddy. "But I'll have to talk to Mommy first. She has to agree to this."

"Okay. Thank you!" I cried.

So Daddy and Mommy talked on the phone. Mommy said I could get my hair cut and have a manicure. Yippee! Daddy said he would pay for my beauty treatment. He even made the appointment for me. I would get my hair cut on Tuesday after school.

That night, I put my teeth under my pillow. Guess what was there when I woke up on Sunday? A barrette! Now how did the Tooth Fairy know I wanted a fancy new blue barrette? I guess because she is magic.

I liked my barrette a lot. But I did not like waiting for Tuesday afternoon. That was very, very hard. Hannie and Nancy both helped make the wait a little easier, though.

On Monday, Nancy said, "Karen, if you want a good haircut, you should find a picture of the style you want and take it to the beauty parlor with you."

"Oh. That's a great idea," I replied. "Thank you." So Nancy and I looked through some magazines until I found a haircut I liked.

"Here! This is it," I said. I cut the picture out of the magazine.

Hannie helped make the wait easier by calling me about her wedding. She called seven times. She kept asking things like, "Do you think I should wear flowers in my hair?" And, "Who should we invite to the wedding?" And, "Do you think your haircut will look good, Karen? I want you to be the most beautiful bridesmaid ever. You'll look pretty, won't you?"

"I hope so," I answered. Boy, did I hope so.

8

Karen's Beauty Treatment

Tuesday *finally* arrived. Mommy picked me up after school. Andrew was with her.

Boo. I did not want my little brother at Gloriana's House of Hair. He would probably wreck something. And I wanted to look like a grown-up person who did not have a four-year-old brother.

I hoped Andrew would sit quietly and behave himself.

Mommy drove downtown. She parked in front of a *very* fancy building. It was mostly glass with a silver-colored door. Bright pink neon lights spelled out Gloriana's House of Hair in script, like this:

Gloriana's House of Hair

"Ooh," I said. "This is so, so beautiful. I bet Gloriana is beautiful, too. She certainly has the most beautiful name I have ever heard. Andrew, you will have to behave yourself. Gloriana's is one of those places where you can't touch anything."

"Don't you worry about Andrew," said Mommy. "I will watch him. If he gets fidgety, we'll take a walk. You won't mind staying in the beauty parlor alone for a few minutes, will you?"

"Oh, no!" I said. (I would feel much more grown-up if that happened.)

Mommy and Andrew and I went inside Gloriana's House of Hair. There were mirrors and pink neon decorations everywhere!

The woman behind the desk said, "Let's

see. Karen Brewer. You're here for a haircut and a manicure, right?"

I nodded.

"Okay. Sally is going to give you the manicure first."

Sally? Darn. I wanted Gloriana to do everything.

"And then," the woman went on, "Gloriana will cut your hair."

Goody!

Mommy and Andrew sat in the waiting area. They looked at magazines.

I followed Sally to her manicure chair. I chose bright pink polish.

When Sally was finished with my nails, she led me to a chair in front of a sink. "Keep your hands very still," she told me. "Your nails are not dry yet."

"Okay," I replied. While my nails dried, a man washed my hair. Then a woman wrapped a towel around my head.

"I'm Gloriana," she said. "Are you ready for your haircut?"

"Yup," I replied. "I even have a picture of what I want." I gave it to Gloriana.

I watched Gloriana while she looked at the picture. I decided I didn't like *Gloriana's* hair at all. Some of it was short, some was long, some was dark, and some was light. But I guessed it didn't matter what Gloriana's hair looked like — as long as she copied the picture and gave me the haircut I wanted.

I sat down in the haircutting chair. I was

so excited, I could feel butterflies in my tummy. Gloriana began to snip away.

The cut I wanted was a nice simple one. I wanted shoulder-length hair (so I could still wear barrettes and hair ribbons in it) with bangs in front.

Gloriana had been cutting my hair for awhile when Mommy came over to me and said, "Andrew is getting wiggly. I'm going to take him for a walk. We'll be back in ten minutes, okay?"

"Okay," I answered.

While Mommy and Andrew were gone, Gloriana kept cutting away. She snipped and cut and cut and snipped. My long hair fell in a pile on the floor.

Suddenly I realized something awful. My hair was getting *too* short! But I was afraid to tell Gloriana.

I wanted Mommy.

By the time Mommy and Andrew came back, Gloriana was finished with my hair. It was not the cut I had asked for.

I was practically bald.

9

The Bride of Frankenstein

Well, okay, I wasn't practically bald, but my hair was *much* shorter than I'd wanted. I had bangs in front, all right, but the rest of my hair was cut close to my head, except for some long hair in the back that did come to my shoulders. It looked really weird. Mostly, my hair was too short for barrettes and ribbons.

When Mommy returned, she looked surprised. "Karen!" she exclaimed. "Is that what you asked for?" She looked suspiciously at Gloriana.

"No," I replied. My lips were quivering.

"It's the latest cut," Gloriana told us. "Karen is very fashionable now."

I didn't care what Gloriana said. I *hated* my hair.

I cried all the way home. (Mommy said my hair would grow back.)

My nails looked great, but with my glasses, my rabbit teeth, my missing teeth, and my horrible, awful hair, I looked worse than ever.

When I woke up the next morning, my stomach did not feel so good. But I knew I just had butterflies again. Only these were not excited butterflies. They were scared butterflies.

How could I face the kids at school? They were all going to tease me. I just knew it. Especially Ricky Torres. Yicky Ricky Torres. He would tease me the worst of all. He would probably call me a mean name.

I was right.

I tried to get to Ms. Colman's room late. I hoped I could slide into my seat just before it was time for the Pledge of Allegiance. But I wasn't late enough. Ms. Colman hadn't even arrived yet. And when I came in, everyone just stared at me. Even Hannie and Nancy.

Then Yicky Ricky said, "Look! Here comes the Bride of Frankenstein!"

He meant *me*.

All the boys and a couple of girls started calling me the Bride of Frankenstein. But

that wasn't the worst thing. The worst thing happened when I ran to the back of the room to be with Hannie and Nancy. (We used to sit together, but after I got my glasses, Ms. Colman moved me to the front row.)

I wanted my friends to make me feel better. Nancy tried. She said, "Karen, your hair is so . . . interesting."

But *Hannie* said, "What *hap*pened?"

"Gloriana didn't copy the picture I gave her," I replied sadly.

Hannie looked thoughtful. Then she said, "I — you — I — Karen, I don't know how to tell you this, but you can't be my bridesmaid. Not while you look like this."

I almost began to cry, but Ms. Colman came into the room then. Everyone sat down. The day began. It was a horrible, long day. I could not think about my work at all. And in the hallway on the way to lunch, two fifth-grade girls pointed at me. That was when I knew for sure that I looked like the Bride of Frankenstein. Fifth-graders *never* pay attention to second-graders. Not unless something is wrong or funny.

I was most upset about Hannie, though. How could she be so mean to me? She was supposed to be one of my best friends.

10

Tiffanie

After school that day, Mommy picked Nancy and me up and drove us home.

As Nancy ran up her driveway, she called, " 'Bye, Karen! See you tomorrow!"

I did not answer her.

"Karen?" said Mommy. "What's wrong? You didn't say a word in the car. Do you feel all right?"

I did not answer Mommy, either.

I marched up to my room. I closed my door. I took Emily Junior out of her cage.

"Emily, Emily, Emily," I said. "Look at

47

me. Do you care if I'm an ugly duckling or the Bride of Frankenstein?"

Emily sniffed around my room. She poked her head into a shoe.

"I guess you don't care," I said. "But you are just a rat. People care. Ricky and his friends teased me, the big kids pointed at me, and one of my very best friends in the world is not my best friend anymore. She won't let me be in her wedding. Just because of my hair. I'm glad you're a rat. Rats are nicer than people."

Sniff, sniff, sniff went Emily Junior. I put her back in her cage.

Then I picked up Goosie, my stuffed cat. I sat on my bed and leaned against the wall. I made Goosie stare at me.

"Well?" I said. "Do *you* think I look like the Bride of Frankenstein?"

I made Goosie nod his head.

"Thanks a lot," I told him.

Then I held him up to my ear. "What? What did you say? . . . That if I can't look

48

beautiful, at least I can have a beautiful name? Boy, that's a great idea, Goosie. Thanks!"

I put Goosie down and thought of beautiful names. Yesterday I had thought Gloriana was a beautiful name, but not today. Not after what Gloriana had done to me. Hmm. Katie? No. Sarah? No. Those were pretty names, but I wanted a *beautiful* name like . . . like Tiffanie! That was a gorgeous name!

At dinner that night I said, "Everybody, I have a new name — "

"How can you have a new name?" interrupted Andrew.

"I just do," I told him. "It's Tiffanie. Isn't that beautiful?"

"It's lovely," said Seth. "Why do you need a new name?"

"I need to pretend I'm beautiful," I replied. "So please remember to call me Tiffanie."

"Okay," agreed Mommy and Seth and Andrew.

But later, Seth said, "Are you finished with your supper, Karen?"

And Andrew said, "Will you play with me, Karen?"

I had to remind both of them that I was Tiffanie.

When I finished my homework that evening, I stood in front of the mirror. I looked at myself from my head to my feet and back again.

I decided I needed more pizzazz. Maybe my new haircut was ugly, and maybe my glasses and teeth were ugly, but I could still try to look glamorous.

So I painted over my pink nail polish.

I put on sparkly gold polish. A friend of Kristy's had given it to me.

There. Now I had a beautiful name and *very* beautiful nails. I was becoming glamorous.

11

"No Way!"

It was time to make a phone call.

I thought I knew just how to get my former best friend back.

"Mommy?" I asked.

Mommy was in the living room reading to Andrew. She was reading *Let's Be Enemies*, which Andrew likes a lot.

"Yes?" replied Mommy.

"May I make a phone call? I need to use the phone in your room so the call will be private."

"Okay," said Mommy.

"Thank you!" I cried. I dashed upstairs and into Mommy and Seth's room. I closed their door.

I dialed Hannie's number. I was excited about my idea.

"Hello, Hannie?" I said, when she answered the phone. "It's me, Karen."

"Oh . . . hi," said Hannie.

"Hannie, I have to tell you something. I am much more beautiful now than I was in school today. I am glamorous. I have a new name — Tiffanie — and I painted my nails sparkly gold. They are the coolest nails in Stoneybrook. So can I be your bridesmaid after all?"

"What did you say your name is?" asked Hannie.

"Tiffanie," I answered. "Um, Tiffanie Titania Brewer."

"And *what* color are your nails?"

"Sparkly gold."

"But your hair and your teeth are still the same?" asked Hannie.

"Yes," I admitted.

"Then you can't be in my wedding," Hannie told me. "No way! I only want a beautiful, *perfect* bridesmaid in my wedding. You are not perfect."

"Oh." I felt like a broken cookie — the one in the package that no one will eat until all the whole ones have been eaten. I couldn't think of anything to say to Hannie except, "Good-bye."

"Good-bye," replied Hannie.

We hung up.

I almost cried. That was how sad I felt. But then I felt something else, too. I was ANGRY! What Hannie was doing was not fair.

After I got into bed that night, I lay awake for a long time. I made plans. I wasn't sure how to be perfect, but I had some ideas for how to be more glamorous.

12

The New Karen

As soon as I woke up the next morning, I hopped out of bed. The first thing I did was check my nails. They looked *perfect*. They were sparkly and gold and I had not chipped one of them.

Then I looked in the mirror. Yuck.

There were my awful teeth and my awful hair. I tried brushing my hair several different ways. That didn't help. My hair looked as awful as ever.

But I said to myself in the mirror, "You are Tiffanie. Tiffanie Titania Brewer. That is a beautiful name. And you can be very glamorous.''

I got dressed. Then I put on five pink plastic bracelets, and eight rings, one on each finger. I get the rings at the dentist's office. On each ring is a different colored stone. When the rings were in place, I put on five necklaces. Then I slipped a stretchy blue beaded bracelet over my foot. Nobody in my class had ever worn an ankle bracelet. I would be the first one.

Boy, was I going to surprise the kids at school.

When Seth dropped me off at school that day, I felt nervous. What would everyone think of the New Karen? I tried to walk into my classroom with confidence. I tried to walk in as if I dressed like this every day.

I sat down at my desk.

I could tell that all the kids were staring at me. I could *feel* their eyes. But no one said a word. That was probably because Yicky Ricky wasn't there yet.

After I had put my things away in my

desk, I walked to the back of the room. A bunch of girls were crowded there.

"Hi," I said.

"Hi," they replied. Well, everyone said hi except Hannie. She wasn't talking to me.

"Guess what. I have a new name," I told the other girls.

Hannie rolled her eyes, but Nancy said, "What is it?"

"It's Tiffanie Titania Brewer."

"Ooh, that's beautiful," said Natalie Springer.

But a few moments later, Nancy said, "Hey, Karen, look what I — "

"My name is *Tiffanie*," I interrupted her.

Just then Ricky came into our classroom. Uh-oh.

"Look, there's the Bride of Frankenstein!" was the first thing Ricky said.

"For your information, Richard, my name is Tiffanie. And by the way, your glasses make you look like an owl," I said loudly.

Everybody laughed. The boys started

hooting at Ricky. "Who-who-who. Who-who-who."

Ricky sat down, looking cross. But he didn't bother me all morning. I think he was afraid I'd call him another name. In fact, Ricky was the only kid in class who remembered *not* to call me Karen.

Natalie said, "I like your nails, Karen."

Jannie Gilbert said, "Sit with me at lunch, Karen."

Nancy said, "I got a new dress, Karen. Come over after school and see it."

"Okay," I replied.

But Ricky said, "You look very, um, pretty, T-Taffy."

"Thank you," I replied, even though he'd gotten the name wrong. At least he had tried.

Hannie didn't call me Tiffanie or Taffy or Karen or anything. She still wasn't speaking to me. I guess it was because I wasn't perfect . . . yet.

13

Krystal

When school was over, Mrs. Dawes, Nancy's mother, picked up Nancy and me and drove us home.

On the way, I said, "Guess what, Mrs. Dawes. I have a new name. It's Tiffanie Titania Brewer. Do you like it?"

"It's . . . very nice," replied Mrs. Dawes.

I saw her glance in the rearview mirror at Nancy and me.

"Hey, Karen — " Nancy began.

"Tiffanie, *Tiffanie*, TIFFANIE!" I cried.

"Sorry," said Nancy. "Hey, Tiffanie, can

you come look at my new dress before you go home?"

"Sure," I replied.

So when we pulled into the Daweses' driveway, I went into Nancy's house. We ran upstairs to her room.

"Here it is," said Nancy. She pulled a beautiful yellow dress out of her closet. "It's for my cousin's bar mitzvah. But first I'm wearing it to the wedding."

"What wedding?" I asked.

"Hannie's."

"Hannie's?!"

"Didn't she invite you?" asked Nancy.

"No," I replied crossly. "She's mad at me and I'm mad at her. Well, I better go. Mommy doesn't know I'm at your house. I'll call you tonight, okay?"

"Okay," replied Nancy. She looked troubled. " 'Bye, Karen."

" 'Bye," I called. I didn't even bother to remind her that my name was Tiffanie.

" 'Bye, Karen," said Mrs. Dawes as I ran through the front door.

" 'Bye, Mrs. Dawes."

Okay, so maybe Tiffanie was a hard name to remember. Maybe it was too different from Karen. By the time I had reached my own house next door, I had decided something. I needed another new and glamorous name, but I needed one that started with the same sound as *Karen*.

All afternoon I thought of names: Camille, Carlotta, Caroline, Catherine, Candace, Clarissa, Cornelia, Kimberly, Kerry, Kelly.

By dinnertime, I had another new name for myself — Krystal. Usually, you spell that name with a C: Crystal. But I would spell it with a K to make it more like Karen.

I told my little-house family my new name.

Seth remembered to call me Krystal!

Mommy forgot and called me Karen.

And Andrew finally called me Tiffanie.

I wasn't going to give up, though. I phoned Nancy that night. "I have another new name," I told her. "It's much easier to remember. My new name is Krystal."

"Krystal," repeated Nancy. Then she said, "Kar — I mean, um, oh well, what's going on with you and Hannie?"

"We're having a fight," I answered. "Hannie says I'm not perfect so I can't be in her wedding. I was going to be her bridesmaid."

"That is so unfair!" exclaimed Nancy.

"Are you going to be mad at Hannie now?" I asked hopefully.

"No," replied Nancy. "I can't be. She

hasn't done anything to me. I'm still Hannie's friend, and I'm still your friend, too."

"Okay. Thanks, Nancy. I mean, thank you for being my friend even when I have ugly hair and ugly teeth."

"You're welcome."

"Good night, Nancy."

"Good night . . . Kristy?"

14

Gazelle, Desirée, and Chantal

The next day, Friday, I went to school as Krystal Karlotta Brewer.

I wore my sparkly gold nail polish and all of my jewelry. And I stuck a secret something in the pocket of my skirt before I left our house. As soon as Seth dropped me off at school, I ran to the girls' room. I set my book bag and my lunch box on the floor. Then I pulled the something out of my pocket.

It was a tube of red lipstick. Mommy had thrown it away while there was still some perfectly good lipstick at the end of the tube. I smeared the lipstick all over my mouth. I did not look exactly the way Mommy does when she wears lipstick, but I looked pretty interesting. Maybe glamorous. One thing was for sure: I was the only second-grader wearing lipstick. And an ankle bracelet.

I marched proudly into my classroom.

Everyone noticed the lipstick right away.

"You're wearing *make*up!" cried Nancy.

"Lipstick!" exclaimed Natalie Springer. "Wow."

(Hannie looked at me, but she did not say anything.)

"Karen — " began Jannie Gilbert.

"Excuse me," I said, "but I have another name. This one is easier to remember. I am now Krystal Karlotta Brewer."

"Christina?" said Natalie.

"No, *Krystal.*"

Nobody could remember Krystal, either (except for Ricky Torres). I gave the kids in my class a whole week to remember it, too. During that time, I found some blusher that

Mommy had thrown away and I started secretly wearing that with the lipstick. My friends were impressed. They thought I was glamorous. Hannie even spoke to me. She said, "You still can't be in my wedding, *Karen*."

After a week I decided I needed another new name. Krystal was not working. So on Monday I told my friends that I was Gazelle. Ricky remembered. He said, "Here's your pencil, Gazelle," when I dropped it on the floor.

But Nancy called me Gardenia and the boys (except for Ricky) called me Godzilla.

I quickly changed my name to Desirée.

Ricky called me Desirée, Natalie called me Dee-Dee, and Nancy, looking confused, called me Dezimay (or something like that).

Hannie called me Karen and said I still couldn't be in her wedding.

That was Wednesday. On Friday, I changed my name to Chantal. I added hair ribbons to my outfit. When I wore just one, it looked funny with my short hair. But when I put

on six at the same time, I looked more glamorous than ever, especially with my nail polish, lipstick, blusher, rings, necklaces, and the ankle bracelet.

In school I announced, "Today I am Chantal Chantilly Brewer."

Ricky called me Chantal, Natalie called me Tiffanie, Nancy called me Rochelle, two boys called me Godzilla again, and three more called me the Bride of Frankenstein.

Hannie still didn't call me anything. She just looked at my outfit and said, "My wedding is on Sunday, and you're not invited."

I said, "I am going to come anyway since I will be at my father's house. And I am going to put on the worst outfit I can think of, and I am going to embarrass you."

Hannie said, "Are not."

I said, "Am too."

Then Ms. Colman said, "Class, please sit down."

So Hannie and I stuck our tongues out at each other and sat down.

The Big Kids

It was that Friday, the day I changed my name to Chantal, that I noticed something. That morning I had looked at myself in the bathroom mirror for a long time, and guess what. My hair was growing out! It was still short, but it looked an awful lot better than it had after Gloriana had first cut it. That was why I had decided to wear the six hair ribbons. My haircut, I decided, was not so bad, no matter what Hannie said.

Guess what else. My teeth looked better,

too. New ones were growing in and filling up the spaces. They had a long way to go, but my mouth looked better without such holes in it. Also, I could tell that the new teeth were going to be bigger than the baby teeth had been. So my front teeth wouldn't look so much like rabbit teeth. They wouldn't stand out as much.

I smiled at myself in the mirror. That made me look even better. I remembered a song from the play *Annie*, and I sang part of it to Goosie when I went back to my bedroom.

"You're never fully dressed without a smile," I sang.

Goosie just stared at me. It is such a shame to have buttons for eyes.

Then Mommy called me. She reminded me that after school, Andrew and I would be going to Daddy's for the weekend.

She did not remember to call me Chantal.

I didn't mind. I was feeling too good on

Friday. I also did not mind much when Hannie and I stuck our tongues out at each other again. Then, something really great happened. It was almost the end of the school day. I had been to the girls' room, and I was walking back to Ms. Colman's class, when I saw two big kids — fifth-grade girls. They were walking toward me. They tried to point at me without my seeing, but I saw anyway.

Uh-oh, I thought. They are going to tease me.

But they didn't. As we passed each other, they smiled at me.

I smiled back.

When the bell rang at the end of the day, I told Nancy what had happened. "You know what?" I said. "I think they liked my hair."

"*Really?*" replied Nancy. I could tell she was impressed. Big kids had liked something about a second-grader!

But Hannie said, "*Sure* they liked your

hair. *Sure* they did." I could tell she didn't believe me.

I did not care what Hannie said. *I* had seen the big kids smile at me. *I* thought they liked my hair. So I felt pretty. (Well, almost pretty.)

16

Hannie's Accident

On Saturday morning I woke up in my room at the big house.

"Good morning, Moosie. Good morning, Tickly," I said.

I lay in bed and wondered what I would do that day. Usually I play with Hannie. But I knew she would not call me. And I certainly would not call her.

At breakfast I announced, "I'm bored."

My whole big-house family was at the kitchen table. I was hoping Kristy would invite me to go shopping with her and her

76

friend Mary Anne. Or that Daddy would say, "Come help me in the garden."

Instead, Elizabeth said, "Why don't you take Emily outside to play. I think she would like that."

Before I could answer her, Andrew said, "Let's teach her to play tag. She doesn't know how. I bet she would like running after us."

"Well . . . okay," I said, even though I thought Emily was too little to understand tag. I didn't want to disappoint Andrew or make Elizabeth cross.

So a few minutes later, Andrew and Emily Michelle and I went into our front yard.

"Keep Emily away from the street," Elizabeth called after us.

"We will," I promised. Then I turned to Emily. I looked into her dark eyes. "Okay," I said, "today you are going to learn how to play a new game. It's called tag."

"Da?" said Emily, pointing to something across the yard.

I looked at Andrew. He shrugged.

"Emily, pay attention," I said. "Now Andrew is going to be It, and he is supposed to run after us. He's supposed to try to catch one of us. Ready? Here we go."

I ran around the front yard. Andrew ran after me. Emily watched us. She laughed.

I stopped. "Emily's not doing anything," I said.

Andrew did not care. He crashed into me. "Tag! You're It!" he cried.

"No fair!" I cried. "I stopped because Emily's not playing."

Andrew was about to argue with me when I noticed something across the street. Hannie was wheeling her bike out of her garage. She hopped onto it, sped down her driveway, lost control, bumped over the curb, and fell in the street.

"Oh, no!" I shouted, just as Hannie wailed, "Ow, ow, ow! Help me!"

I forgot that Hannie and I were mad at each other. I ran to the sidewalk. Luckily, no cars were coming, so I dashed across the

street. I helped move Hannie and her bicycle
onto the Papadakises' front lawn.

Then I helped Hannie inside to her mother.

Hannie's mouth was bleeding all over the
place. She spit two teeth into her hand.

"Oh, *Mom*my!" sobbed Hannie. *"Look!"*

"It's okay," said Mrs. Papadakis calmly.
She told Hannie to rinse her mouth out at
the kitchen sink. "They were baby teeth
and they were loose anyway."

"I know," said Hannie. But she could not stop crying.

Her mother gave her a hug. She washed Hannie's face.

Hannie was still crying.

"Does your mouth hurt a lot?" asked Mrs. Papadakis.

"No," replied Hannie. "Not much. But now I am too ugly to marry Scott."

17

Scott and Hannie

After Hannie stopped crying I went back to my house. I was sorry Hannie had hurt herself, and I was sorry she thought she was ugly. But I did not want to stay with her. Hannie had been mean to me for almost two weeks. She had not said, "I'm sorry," to me. She had not even thanked me for helping her when she fell off her bike.

Daddy didn't know about that, though. And the first thing he said when I came back from the Papadakises' was, "How is

Hannie? Andrew told me about her accident."

"She's okay," I replied. "She knocked out two of her teeth, but they were baby teeth and they were already loose."

"Hannie must be feeling pretty bad, though."

I shrugged. "I guess so."

"I'm surprised you're not keeping Hannie company. You two are always together. Well, you can visit her after lunch," said Daddy.

"Do I have to?" I asked.

"Don't you want to?"

"I guess," I answered. I didn't feel like telling Daddy about our fight.

So after lunch I had to go back to Hannie's house.

Boy, was I relieved when Scott Hsu arrived at Hannie's at the same time I did! Now I would not have to face Hannie by myself.

"Hi, Scott," I said.

"Hi, Karen," he answered. He rang the
doorbell.

Linny let us inside. "Hannie's up in her
room," he said.

Scott ran up the stairs to Hannie's bedroom. I followed slowly. What was I supposed to say to Hannie? Sorry you knocked
your teeth out — now you look as ugly as
I do? Sorry you've been a pain in the neck?
Sorry Gloriana is a rotten haircutter?

At least I was still looking pretty good. When I got dressed that morning I hadn't put on hair ribbons or jewelry or anything. I had just brushed my hair out. And I looked . . . nice.

Scott had reached Hannie's room. I was trailing behind him, but I could hear him say, "Karen's here, too."

I took a deep breath. I entered Hannie's room.

She was lying on her bed, reading a book. She looked sad.

"I heard about your accident," Scott told Hannie.

(I didn't say anything. I just stood inside the doorway.)

"You did?" said Hannie in a small voice.

Scott nodded. "Andrew Brewer told me." (Had he told the whole world?) "Well, I was just wondering," Scott went on. "Will you feel well enough to have the wedding tomorrow?"

Hannie shook her head. "You don't want to marry me now," she said. "Look at me."

She opened her mouth and showed Scott the two gaps where her teeth had been.

"So what?" said Scott.

"I'm not perfect. I'm *ugly!*" cried Hannie.

Scott's eyes widened. "I don't care what you look like," he said. "I'm not marrying your *face*. I'm marrying *you*. Okay?"

"Okay," said Hannie. She smiled a tiny smile.

Scott left then. As he ran down the hall, he called over his shoulder, "See you tomorrow at our wedding!"

I put my hand on my hip and stared at Hannie.

She could not look back at me.

18

"I'm Sorry, Chandrelle"

Since Hannie could not look at me, or even say anything, finally *I* said, "My father made me come over here. I didn't want to, but he said I had to."

At last Hannie glanced up. "I guess if I were you, I wouldn't have wanted to come over, either."

"You've been pretty mean to me," I told her.

Hannie nodded. "I can't believe how nice Scott was to me. I'm sorry I've been mean, Chandrelle."

"It's Chantal," I replied. (Wouldn't *any-body* *ever* get my name right?)

"Chantal," Hannie repeated. She paused. "You know what I've been thinking ever since I fell off my bike?"

"What?" I said. I sat on the edge of Hannie's bed.

"I've been thinking," Hannie began, "that you must have been feeling awfully bad the last couple of weeks. It's terrible to think you look ugly. It's even worse to think people won't like you because of that."

"It *was* bad," I said. "It was bad when I looked in the mirror, and it was bad when the boys called me the Bride of Frankenstein. But you know what was the worst of all?"

"What?" asked Hannie.

"When you told me I couldn't be in your wedding because I wasn't perfect."

Hannie lowered her eyes. "I know that was unfair. I'm not sure why I did that. I guess I just wanted the wedding to be . . . perfect. But I figured something out this morning. And I'm really glad you came over

because now I can tell you about it. I figured
out that just because I didn't like your teeth
and hair didn't mean I couldn't like *you*.
Remember what Scott said? He said, 'I'm
not marrying your *face*. I'm marrying *you*.'
That's the same thing. Anyway, I guess
*no*body's perfect."

"That's what Daddy always says," I told
Hannie. I smiled at her.

"I know," she replied. "My parents say
the same thing."

"Do you think it's true?" I asked.

"What? That nobody's perfect?" said Hannie.

"Yes."

Hannie looked thoughtful. "Yup," she said finally. "I do think that's true, Chantal. . . . Hey! I got your name right!"

I giggled. "You can call me Karen now."

"I can? Why?"

"Because I don't think I need fancy things anymore. I'm not wearing my hair ribbons or my jewelry. See? And you just said you like me even if I'm not perfect. So I don't have to be glamorous, either. I can just be Karen Brewer again."

"Good," said Hannie. "I like Karen Brewer better than Chantal and Tiffanie and all those other names. Um, do you still want to be in my wedding?"

"Of course I do!"

"Oh, great! Gosh, we have to figure out what you're going to wear."

"How about my pink party dress?" I said. "And my party shoes."

"Perfect. You can put flowers in your hair, just like me. Gosh, I better remember to pick them."

"What else do you have to do?" I asked.

"Oh, lots of things."

For almost an hour, Hannie and I sat in her room. We talked about her wedding.

19

Hannie's Wedding

The next day was wedding day! That morning I didn't lie around in my bed. I leaped up! The wedding was going to be at eleven o'clock, and I had to be ready. First I ate breakfast. Usually I get dressed first, but I did not want to spill orange juice or cereal on my party dress.

As soon as breakfast was over I put on my pink dress, my white socks with the rosebuds on them, and my party shoes. I brushed my hair. Then I looked at myself in the long mirror in Daddy and Elizabeth's room. I decided I looked almost . . . pretty.

I checked my watch. Ten-thirty.

"Hey, wedding time!" I yelled. "Come on, David Michael." David Michael was going to be the minister.

We ran out the front door. Kristy would be coming over later with Emily and Andrew. They would be wedding guests.

When we reached the Papadakises' backyard, David Michael and I found Hannie and Linny (who was going to be the best man) and Sari. Sari is Hannie's little sister. She is Emily's age. She was going to be the flower girl.

Boy, did Hannie look pretty. She was wearing high-heeled shoes and her mother's wedding dress. She had to hold the dress up high so she wouldn't step on it, but that was okay.

Sari looked pretty, too, but I knew she had no idea what was going on. And Linny and David Michael looked handsome in their suits. They looked cross, though. That was because they hate wearing suits.

92

"Hi, Karen!" called Hannie when she saw me. "Come here! I've got our flowers!"

Hannie had picked dandelions. She poked them into our hair. I hoped they wouldn't fall out.

"Where's Scott?" I asked.

"He's . . ." said Hannie slowly, looking around, "right there!" Walking proudly into the Papadakises' yard were Scott and his older brother. They were both wearing suits, only they didn't look cross. Scott was grinning.

"Is everyone here?" I asked.

"Everyone but the guests," Hannie replied.

The guests arrived in bunches — Kristy, Andrew, Emily, Nancy, some kids from down the street, Scott's parents, and Hannie's parents.

Hannie's mother was carrying a camera. She was the wedding photographer.

When everyone had arrived, Hannie said, "Let's get started. Sari, throw your flower petals. Daddy, the music."

Sari was holding a basket full of bits of tissue paper. She flung the entire basket onto the ground. Everyone laughed. Sari cried. Her father had to pick her up. But first he turned on a tape deck. Hannie wanted to get married to the tape of "Take Me Out to the Ball Game." It's her favorite song.

Scott and Hannie stood in front of David Michael, the minister. Linny and I stood sort of behind them. I was not sure what the bridesmaid and the best man were supposed to do.

"Okay," said David Michael. "Um, let's see. We are gathered here today for this wedding. This wedding of Hannie and Scott."

Click, went Mrs. Papadakis's camera.

"Hannie, do you take Scott to be your husband?" asked David Michael.

"I do," said Hannie seriously.

"Scott, do you take Hannie to be your wife?"

"I do," said Scott. Then he whispered loudly, "Linny, we need the rings."

94

Linny had not been paying attention. He jumped a mile. Then he put his hand in his pocket and pulled out two of my dentist rings. I had lent them to Hannie the day before.

Scott took the rings. He gave one to Hannie. She slipped it onto Scott's finger, and Scott slipped the other ring onto Hannie's finger.

"Okay!" cried David Michael. "You guys are married! You can kiss."

"No way!" shrieked Scott and Hannie at the same time.

Click, click, click went the camera.

All the guests cheered.

A Wedding for Karen?

On Monday morning I woke up in my bed at Mommy's. I was feeling happy, even though I was sorry my weekend at Daddy's was over. I was sorry the wedding was over, too. That had been fun.

But I was happy to be regular old Karen Brewer again. I did not need sparkly nail polish. I did not need Mommy's makeup. I did not need necklaces and the ankle bracelet or my hair ribbons. I did not even need a new name.

I got dressed quickly. Dressing went much faster when I only had to put on clothes. Then I brushed my hair. I looked at myself in the mirror. I examined my teeth and my haircut. My teeth were growing in and my hair was growing out.

Perfect.

At school that day, two very amazing things happened.

The first one happened after Seth had dropped me off at school and I was walking to the front door. I passed those two big fifth-grade girls who had smiled at me, and guess what. (You won't believe this.) They had gotten their hair cut just like mine! Honest.

I ran to Ms. Colman's room.

"Hannie! Nancy!" I cried. (Ms. Colman wasn't there yet, so nobody reminded me to use my indoor voice.)

"What? What is it?" exclaimed my friends.

"Those two big kids, those girls I told you about on Friday — "

"The ones who smiled at you?" interrupted Nancy.

"Yes," I replied. "Well, they got haircuts like mine! I swear it. I just saw them."

Nancy's eyes grew wide. So did Hannie's.

"You — you started something that the big kids *copied*," said Hannie in awe. "Wow . . ."

The second amazing thing happened on the playground that day. Our class was crowded around Hannie. Everyone wanted to know about her wedding.

"Are you *really married*?" asked Natalie.

"Well . . . no," replied Hannie. "David Michael isn't a real minister. But Scott and I can pretend. He is my best boyfriend."

"Did you get wedding presents?" asked Jannie.

"No, but I have a wedding *ring*." Hannie held her hand out. On it was the dentist ring. It was gold with a red jewel. I had decided to let Scott and Hannie keep the rings.

"My bridesmaid," Hannie went on, "was Karen. She was dressed up. She looked very beautiful."

"Thank you," I said. "Hannie looked beautiful, too. She was wearing her mother's *real* wedding dress."

"Oooh," said a whole bunch of kids.

"My mother took pictures at the wedding," said Hannie. "I'll bring them to school when they've been developed."

Just then I felt someone tug at my arm. I turned around. Yicky Ricky was behind me.

"Hey, Chantal," he whispered. "Come here." He pulled me away from the crowd of kids. "Chantal," he said again, "I was wondering. *Some*day, would you maybe *think* about marrying me? Maybe?"

Ricky wanted to marry *me?*

I looked at him. I could tell he was serious. He was even a little nervous.

Still, I almost said, "No." After all, this

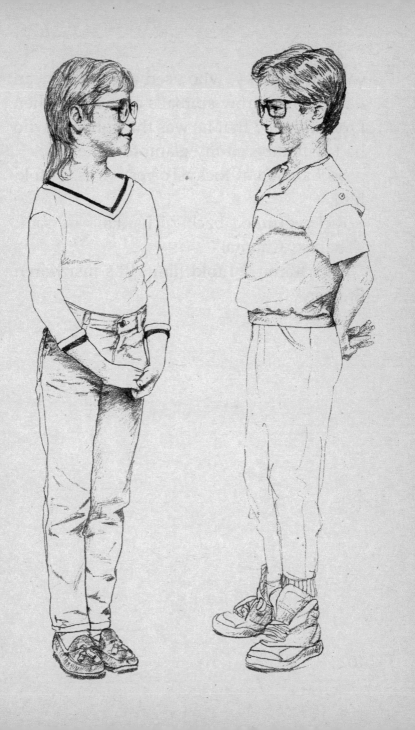

was Yicky Ricky, who used to call me mean names and throw spitballs at me. But then I remembered that he was the only one who had remembered my glamorous names.

So I smiled at Ricky Torres. "Yes," I told him.

Ricky grinned back. "Thanks," he said. "Thanks, Chantal."

"It's Karen," I told him. "It's just Karen Brewer."

About the Author

ANN M. MARTIN lives in New York City and loves animals. Her cat, Mouse, knows how to take the phone off the hook.

Other books by Ann M. Martin that you might enjoy are *Stage Fright*, *Me and Katie (the Pest)*, and the books in *The Baby-sitters Club* series.

Ann likes ice cream, the beach, and *I Love Lucy*. And she has her own little sister, whose name is Jane.

Little Sister

Don't miss #9

KAREN'S SLEEPOVER

My friends and I put our sleeping bags on the floor in the playroom. We arranged them in a circle, like the spokes of a wagon wheel.

Then we sat on our sleeping bags. We opened our overnight bags.

"Look what I brought!" cried Leslie. She held up her nightgown. It had leopard spots and red fringe on it.

We started to laugh.

"I brought — ta-dah! — my musical puppy," said Jannie. "Look. You push this button on his tummy and he moves his head. Plus, his eyes blink on and off, and a music box inside him plays 'How Much Is That Doggie in the Window?' "

Now we couldn't stop laughing.

My sleepover had started.

Little Sister™

by Ann M. Martin, author of *The Baby-sitters Club* ®

More Titles... 👉

The Baby-sitters Little Sister titles continued...

☐	MQ44825-0	#29 Karen's Cartwheel	$2.75
☐	MQ45645-8	#30 Karen's Kittens	$2.75
☐	MQ45646-6	#31 Karen's Bully	$2.95
☐	MQ45647-4	#32 Karen's Pumpkin Patch	$2.95
☐	MQ45648-2	#33 Karen's Secret	$2.95
☐	MQ45650-4	#34 Karen's Snow Day	$2.95
☐	MQ45652-0	#35 Karen's Doll Hospital	$2.95
☐	MQ45651-2	#36 Karen's New Friend	$2.95
☐	MQ45653-9	#37 Karen's Tuba	$2.95
☐	MQ45655-5	#38 Karen's Big Lie	$2.95
☐	MQ45654-7	#39 Karen's Wedding	$2.95
☐	MQ47040-X	#40 Karen's Newspaper	$2.95
☐	MQ47041-8	#41 Karen's School	$2.95
☐	MQ47042-6	#42 Karen's Pizza Party	$2.95
☐	MQ46912-6	#43 Karen's Toothache	$2.95
☐	MQ47043-4	#44 Karen's Big Weekend	$2.95
☐	MQ47044-2	#45 Karen's Twin	$2.95
☐	MQ47045-0	#46 Karen's Baby-sitter	$2.95
☐	MQ43647-3	Karen's Wish Super Special #1	$2.95
☐	MQ44834-X	Karen's Plane Trip Super Special #2	$3.25
☐	MQ44827-7	Karen's Mystery Super Special #3	$2.95
☐	MQ45644-X	Karen's Three Musketeers Super Special #4	$2.95
☐	MQ45649-0	Karen's Baby Super Special #5	$3.25
☐	MQ46911-8	Karen's Campout Super Special #6	$3.25

Available wherever you buy books, or use this order form.

- -

Scholastic Inc., P.O. Box 7502, 2931 E. McCarty Street, Jefferson City, MO 65102

Please send me the books I have checked above. I am enclosing $ _____
(please add $2.00 to cover shipping and handling). Send check or money order - no cash
or C.O.Ds please.

Name _____ Birthdate _____

Address _____

City _____ State/Zip _____

Please allow four to six weeks for delivery. Offer good in U.S.A. only. Sorry, mail orders are not
available to residents to Canada. Prices subject to change.   BLS793